SHARING IS CARING

by: CLAYBIGMAC

Gotham Books
30 N Gould St.
Ste. 20820, Sheridan, WY 82801
https://gothambooksinc.com/

Phone: 1 (307) 464-7800

© 2022 Claybigmac. All rights reserved.
No part of this book may be reproduced, stored in a retrieval system, or transmitted by any means without the written permission of the author.

Published by Gotham Books (November 10, 2022)

ISBN: 979-8-88775-134-4 (sc)
ISBN: 979-8-88775-135-1 (e)

Because of the dynamic nature of the Internet, any web addresses or links contained in this book may have changed since publication and may no longer be valid.

The views expressed in this work are solely those of the author and do not necessarily reflect the views of the publisher, and the publisher hereby disclaims any responsibility for them.

FRIENDS

A true friend never stops caring for what they see in you,
true friends see you not with their eyes,
but with their heart.
A true friend will see you from the inside out.

"Happiness begins in the Heart!" ~ Claybigmac

Would you care for a bear,
if it gave you a stare?
Could you go near a bear,
or would it give you a scare?

What about sharing a house with a blue mouse, or even seeing that blue mouse live in a tree house?
How much would you care if you had to share?

Would you help a small snail
who was lost or of trail,
even help a red whale to
save her own tail?

What about sharing a friendly smile with a crocodile, if he asked you to stay and talk for a while?

You could even share the tale of how you saved that red whale.

If you see a skunk that`s pink,
please stop and have a think
for if a skunk was pink,
would it smell or even stink?

Could you hold an elephant's trunk,
away from that pink skunk,
in case the skunk it stunk and shrunk
the elephant's trunk?

Do you think this shows you care about that monkey in the chair?

Could you take a photograph of
a spotty tall giraffe
who signed an autograph while
letting out a laugh?

If you see a grumpy drake,
please do not take his cake.
This could be a big mistake,
as he might chase you to the lake.

But still share that photograph of the spotty tall giraffe.

I'm sure you will agree,
be the best that you can be.
So, tell not one or two, but much,
much more than three. That when you start
to share you really show you care.

Yes, sharing shows you care,
but please be all aware,
that caring is the key and
the best part is it`s free.

Reflection Time

1. Have you ever shared something with a friend, what was it?

   Answer: _____

2. How does sharing with other people show you care for them?

   Answer: _____

3. Think of someone who has cared for you. How did that make you feel?

   Answer: _____

4. Why is it important to care for other people?

   Answer: _____

5. Who do you care about and why?

   Answer: _____

"Happiness begins in the Heart!" ~ Claybigmac

www.ingramcontent.com/pod-product-compliance
Lightning Source LLC
LaVergne TN
LVHW072131060526
838201LV00071B/5011